SEP - - 2015

MW00889771

LAKE BLUFF PUBLIC LIBRARY
123 Scranton Avenue
Lake Bluff, IL 60044

GINNY LOUISE

AND THE SCHOOL SHOWDOWN

by Tammi Sauer

illustrated by Lynn Munsinger

DISNEP • HYPERION

Los Angeles   New York

Text copyright © 2015 by Tammi Sauer

Illustrations copyright © 2015 by Lynn Munsinger

All rights reserved. Published by Disney • Hyperion, an imprint of Disney Book Group. No part of this book may be reproduced or transmitted in any form or by any means, electronic or mechanical, including photocopying, recording, or by any information storage and retrieval system, without written permission from the publisher. For information address Disney • Hyperion, 125 West End Avenue, New York, New York 10023.

First Edition, June 2015

10 9 8 7 6 5 4 3 2 1

H106-9333-5-15060

Printed in Malaysia

Library of Congress Cataloging-in-Publication Data

Sauer, Tammi.

Ginny Louise and the school showdown / by Tammi Sauer ;

illustrated by Lynn Munsinger.—First U.S. edition.

pages cm

Summary: "Ginny Louise stands up to bullying by the Truman Elementary Troublemakers and wins them over with her unwavering cheerfulness"—Provided by publisher.

ISBN 978-1-4231-6853-9

[1. Bullying—Fiction. 2. Schools—Fiction.] I. Munsinger, Lynn, illustrator. II. Title.

PZ7.S2502Gi 2015

[E]—dc23   2014025012

Designed by Maria Elias

Reinforced binding

Visit www.DisneyBooks.com

For the Marlow Elementary Outlaws

—T.S.

The Truman Elementary Troublemakers were a bad bunch.

Especially these three:

Day after day, these scoundrels made waves.

They dodged danger.

And in the classroom?

You don't even want to *know* what went on.

This scowly, growly crowd grew
badder and badder until . . .

"Hi, everybody! I'm Ginny Louise!"

Ginny Louise did not scowl.

She did not growl.

And she warmed the heart
of her teacher.

Make-My-Day May had only one thing to say:
"Yer gonna pay."

"I'd *love* to stay! Thanks, new best friend!"

(Truth be told, Ginny Louise only ever heard what she wanted to.)

All morning long,
Ginny Louise painted.

whoosh
whoosh
whoosh

la-la-la

And sang.

scritch
scritch
scritch

And **learned** things.

Destructo Dude found this as appealing
as cooties on a cape.

"You're messing with my bad-guy force field!"

"Yer sweetness makes me seasick!"
said Cap'n Catastrophe.

Make-My-Day May had only one thing to say:

"Yer gonna pay."

"I'd *love* to play!" said Ginny Louise.
"You're the *best* new best friend!"

All around the playground, Ginny Louise
skipped and whooped and floopity-flooped.

Cap'n Catastrophe found her as welcome as barnacles on a booty.

He told her to walk the plank.

Destructo Dude demanded she go to a galaxy far, far away.

And when Ginny Louise didn't help
swipe all the toys from the sandbox?
Make-My-Day May didn't know *what* to say.

After recess, Ginny Louise made a special delivery.
"Pardon me. I believe these belong to you."

Make-My-Day May found this as pleasing as ticks in a taco.

She huffed over to Ginny Louise. She planted her boots. And she gave that girl the *stink eye*.

"Varmint," said May, "it's time for a showdown."

"I'd love a *hoedown*!"

"I SAID *SHOWDOWN*!" hollered May.

But Ginny Louise didn't seem to notice. (Or care.)

"I call this first song
'Hooray for May.'"

"May is the best friend ev-er.
She's so pretty.
She's not fake.
I love her more than
chocolate cake."

"Shiver me timbers!
That hurts me ears!" said
Cap'n Catastrophe.

"Where's an escape hatch
when I need one?" said
Destructo Dude.

Everyone turned to May.

Her lip twitched. Her fingers itched. Then . . .

She couldn't resist.
"What the hey!" said May.
"Yippie-ki-yay!"

Soon *everybody* joined in.

Hats flung.
Lights swung.
Floorboards sprung.

"Aha!" said the teacher.
"FREEZE!"

"Excuse me, but the freezing kind of ruins
our hoedown," said Ginny Louise.

The teacher was a mite confused.
None of the scowly faces on the wanted
posters matched anyone in *this* crowd.

"Dagnabbit!" cried the teacher.
"Where ARE those pesky troublemakers?!"

"They went away," said May.
"But *we'll* stay."

Ever since, the students at Truman Elementary
were a pretty good bunch.

But they *still* had their moments.

"Make my day," said May.

And everybody did.

Especially Ginny Louise.